MY MOLLY (DEPARTED)

2

MY MOLLY (DEPARTED)

Talan Memmott

UNDERACADEMY
COLLEGE

FREE DOGMA
2014

First Printing: 2014

ISBN 978-0-9885983-2-4

UnderAcademy College / Free Dogma Press

PREVOCATIONS

[1]"All moanday, tearsday, wailsday, thumpsday, frightday, shatterday till the fear of the Law." [JJ]

[2]"Alone! Alone! Alone!" [AS]

[3]"What could be more convincing ... than the gesture of laying one's cards face up on the table?" [JL]

[4]"But curb thou the high spirit in thy breast, for gentle ways are best, and keep aloof from sharp contentions." [H]

[5]"The only thing you must never speak of is your happiness." [SB]

[6]"Words empty as the wind are best left unsaid." [H]

[7]"I dream, therefore I exist." [AS]

[8]"Dreams are manifestations of identities." [KA]

[9]"Everything is possible, everything, even the most sordid and undignified things." [RW]

[10]"Naturally, Love's the most distant possibility." [GB]

[11]"I don't like books with a Molly in them" [JJ]

[12]"...you would do better, at least no worse, to obliterate texts than to blacken margins, to fill in the holes of words till all is black and flat and the whole ghastly business looks like what it is, senseless, speechless, issueless misery." [SB]

[13]"People are constantly clamoring for the joy of life. As for me, I find the joy of life in the hard and cruel battle of life - to learn something is a joy to me." [AS]

[14]"Every bond ... is a bond to sorrow." [JJ]

[15] "Better hope deferred than none." [SB]

[16]"I wept not, so to stone within I grew." [DA]

[17]"In the face of what's hopeless there can only be despair!" [AS]

[18]"Nothing is funnier than unhappiness, I grant you that." [SB]

[19]"There is no greater sorrow than to recall happiness in times of misery" [DA]

[20]"truth has only one face: that of a violent contradiction." [GB]

[21]"Our vulgar perception is not concerned with other than vulgar phenomena." [SB]

[22]"People who keep dogs are cowards who haven't got the guts to bite people themselves." [AS]

[23]"geometry implies the heterogeneity of locus, namely that there is a locus of the Other." [JL]

[24]"wrote over every square inch of the only foolscap available" [JJ]

[25]"Nothing happens, nobody comes, nobody goes, it's awful." [SB]

[26]"indifferent, paring his fingernails." [JJ]

[27]"From a little spark may burst a flame." [DA]

[28]"Love is a haunting melody that I have never mastered, and I fear I never will." [WB]

[29]"Man goes constantly in fear of himself. His erotic urges terrify him." [GB]

[30]"Will cannot be quenched against its will." [DA]

[31]"Necessity knows no rules." [AS]

[32]"Crime hides, and by far the most terrifying things are those which elude us." [GB]

[33]"Writings scatter to the winds blank checks in an insane charge." [JL]

[34]"A man's errors are his portals of discovery." [JJ]

[35]"I love to doubt as well as know." [DA]

[36]"We are plagiarists, liars and criminals." [KA]

[37]"Remember tonight... for it is the beginning of always." [DA]

[38]"and yes I said yes I will Yes" [JJ]

[39]"In youth and beauty, wisdom is but rare!" [H]

[40]"That is all very senseless, but this senselessness has a pretty mouth, and it smiles." [RW]

[41]"Happiness consumes itself like a flame. It cannot burn forever, it must go out, and the presentiment of its end destroys it at its very peak." [AS]

[42]"After the event, even a fool is wise." [H]

[43]"Let us not speak of them; but look, and pass on." [DA]

[44]"silence, cunnning, and exile." [JJ]

[45]"In silence you can't hide anything ... as you can in words." [AS]

[46]"What other knowledge will my solitude and muteness bring? What other worlds?" [KA]

[47]"No one wanted him; he was outcast from life's feast." [JJ]

[48]"Life has always taken place in a tumult without apparent cohesion" [GB]

[49]"Decidedly it will never have been given to me to finish anything, except perhaps breathing. One must not be greedy." [SB]

[50]"The narration, in fact, doubles the drama with a commentary without which no mise en scene would be possible." [JL]

[51]"Every word is like an unnecessary stain on silence and nothingness" [SB]

[52]"The bitter dregs of Fortune's cup to drain." [H]

[53]"The mocker is never taken seriously when he is most serious" [JJ]

[54]"Pride, envy, avarice…" [DA]

[55]"No pen, no ink, no table, no room, no time, no quiet, no inclination." [JJ]

[56]"Once a certain degree of insight has been reached, all men talk, when talk they must, the same tripe." [SB]

[57]"If you ask me what I want, I'll tell you. I want everything." [KA]

[58]"We walk through ourselves, meeting robbers, ghosts, giants, old men, young men, wives, widows, brothers..." [JJ]

[59]"Before our eyes, at least before mine (not hers, perhaps), everything was veiled in impenetrable darkness." [RW]

[60]"History ... is a nightmare from which I am trying to awake" [JJ]

[61]"past moments old dreams back again" [SB]

[62]"Abandon hope, all ye who enter here." [DA]

[63]"That's how it is on this bitch of an earth." [SB]

[64]"One by one they we're all becoming shades." [JJ]

[65]"Personally I have no bone to pick with graveyards" [SB]

[66]"this timecoloured place where we live in our paroqial fermament one tide on another" [JJ]

[67]"Habit is a great deadener." [SB]

[68]"Sorrow has the fortunate peculiarity that it preys upon itself." [AS]

[69]"Don't touch me! Don't question me! Don't speak to me! Stay with me!" [SB]

[70]"exagmination round ... factification for incamination of a warping process." [JJ]

[71]"Some people seem to be born to suffer." [AS]

[72]"Every man has inside himself a parasitic being who is acting not at all to his advantage." [WB]

[73]"We must overact our part in some measure, in order to produce any effect at all." [DA]

[74]"I can't go on. I'll go on." [SB]

[75]"The sovereign being is burdened with a servitude that crushes him" [GB]

[76]"Uncouth tongues, horrible shriekings of despair,
Shrill and faint voices, cries of pain and rage…" [DA]

[77]"Love letter or conspiratorial letter, letter of betrayal
or letter of mission, letter of summons or letter of
distress…" [JL]

[78]"Sentimentality is unearned emotion." [JJ]

[79]"In deep sadness there is no place for sentimentality."
[WB]

[80]"There I sat, in the biting wind, wishing she were
gone." [SB]

[81]"nothing can be grasped, destroyed, or burnt, except
in a symbolic way, as one says, in effigy, in absentia."
[JL]

[82]"Be just and if you can't be just, be arbitrary." [WB]

[83]"The will … is the driving force of the mind. If it's
injured, the mind falls to pieces." [AS]

[84]"There is a time for many words, and there is also a
time for sleep." [H]

[85]"all these calculations yes explanations yes the whole story from beginning to end yes completely false yes" [SB]

[86]"What does it matter how many lovers you have if none of them gives you the universe?" [JL]

[87]"To find a form that accommodates the mess, that is the task of the artist now." [SB]

[88]"Longest way round is the shortest way home." [JJ]

[89]"A judgment about life has no meaning except the truth of the one who speaks last." [GB]

[90]" Try again. Fail again. Fail better." [SB]

[91]"I leave my duffel in the grass." [TM]

Week One

Thursday:

(

Monday:

Misfortune begins mistakes are made transgression loss of
restraint unknown *patterns*
indistinguishable from emergent crests and falls crest and fall
to stay blue lifts the lonely leaves leads again the impossible
patterns
to haunt to haunt to haunt. The next so sweet. And then. The
impossibility of next so sweet never so sweet never again
against the broken *patterns*
dilapidated commotion severe longing to haunt forced sweet
belligerent and corporeal estimation hope cynical hopeless
with softness soft *patterns*
soft hopelessness commutes suppressed crushed trying

17

climbing up and out down to hope. To hope away from
patterns
lurching moments

Monday:

Finally finality fatality of longing unknown *patterns*
and disbelief still *patterns*
severe longing incoherent *patterns*
to haunt to haunt to haunt. Chirping.

Twittering impossible wails wells to haunt to haunt to crush
the uncanny twittering otherly utterly meeting outside of
severe *patterns*

 out of time longing still despite movement dilapidated toward
the otherly toward the otherly toward the otherly. To haunt to
haunt to die in severe longing for dead disinterest my molly.
My molly my molly my memory bent *patterns*

click click click

Wednesday:

And trying to think ahead placeless without already without
patterns

conditions forgot to forgot to forgot to. Determined. Severe
longing *patterns*
fade face leading moments tracing movements tracking
tripping over departure toward the impossibility of next so
sweet never so sweet my molly my molly my molly. Departure
departed silence before *patterns*
too too to misunderstand crushing misunderstood *patterns*
severe poetry. And listless

Tuesday:

Wicker pigs wander hazy forgotten *patterns*
buried dead my molly departed beatrice arriving late
unchecked severe longing denies time out of time played by
untimeliness against my molly departs again arriving early too
late drinking Tivoli twittering again tomorrow castles snow
forgotten unchecked *patterns*
weakened beatrice remembering and absent my molly my
molly not my molly forced

click click click

Clacking desperate the hand the finger the tongue the wordless
misfortune again beatrice begins my molly sweeping
congestion

clack clack clack

Jittery

Friday:

Start staring nomadic mindful tasks another continent fateful
patterns
moments too much faith new unknown *patterns*
severe longing snow light hardened *patterns*
my molly to haunt to haunt to haunt. Leaving moments
finding losing face magnetic before not the truth dark matter
patterns
not the truth not severe severed longing chirping haunts and
too sweet rising poetry twittering my molly twittering my
molly

Thursday:

Else back again another continent my molly my molly my
molly. Homeward old *patterns*
to haunt severe longing emerges cannot emerges will not
emerges swollen sadness severe *patterns*
onward to haunt to haunt to haunt. Chirping. Played by time
rushed unknown urgency *patterns*
my molly my molly longing twittering crushed to haunt to
haunt to haunt disinterest

20

Appendix A.

We are leaving for St. Petersburg by ferry. There's no other way to get there from here, so we are leaving by ferry. The flight has been delayed so we'll take the ferry. The ferry is fogged in so we'll travel by train. There's no other way to get to Pittsburgh from here. The train to St. Pittsburgh has been delayed so we'll take the ferry. We won't depart at all.

The traffic -- vehicular and pedestrian, passes by the two arched windows bordered in Avocado. The white wall between the arches breaks pedestrian strides, the drive from frame to frame, slipping horizontal... A Number-One bus passes by, cars park, headlights and streetlights switch on or off. From here I can read *swedcowayne'scoffeekinobarmat*... Compiled in the moment as I pass my eye from one frame to the next... There is other signage I can't quite read, outside ... something in blue, and in white -- the number 495 surrounded by a field of lavender.

These are the problems of the moment: at this moment, these are the problems of all matter, all that matters, everything material and immaterial -- these are the problems.

Impermanence and dislocation: thinking time, too much time to think about too little time. Thinking ahead ... to ...

21

thinging the thinking. Now. What is *not yet* remains the promise.

The promise: filled and willed by the promise. The premonition. Before. The melancholy that is the foundation of all pre-tended joy. This is the promise.

F
Falling.
l
l
i
n
g
   down.
         The willing.
Willing movement
toward the willing.
Then, the thing.
              Something,
then,
         some-body.

We didn't do this because you are drunk,
I am.
I didn't will this because we are drunk,
I am.

We, we, we, we, we.
Us, us, us, us, us.
You, me, me, me, me.

Did we?

Appendix B.

Her dress is ragged and torn
standing undisturbed

I will teach you a lesson

the wet dog will read your fortune now
secret agent of the stars

You will hear me

tired and dirty
bitter blinded ragamuffin

this channel smells of ...

vanilla beans and mildew

this channel smells of ...

butter cream and human sweat

this channel smells of ...

Brussels sprouts and peppermint

this channel smells of ...

cinnamon and rotting fish

Week Two

Sunday:

Don't want to be to be to be. Backward elder *patterns*
severe longing needs beyond before my molly emerges to
haunt to haunt to haunt the ponds and glance graze the wicker
sweeping over carved figures over between identical alders to
haunt to haunt to haunt. Standing silent speaking waiting
hopeless in cynical hope to feel *patterns*
wasted time out of time played by time. Tattered wicker. My
molly flickers dies diminishes *patterns*
hopeless weakness to haunt corporeal slap slap slap. Chirping.
New *patterns*
hope returns cynical colored by time played by time out of
time. Chirping. Tattooed finality fatality severe longing to
haunt to haunt my molly my molly *patterns*
cobblestone umbrella stumble limp lurching crushed

click click click

Thursday:

Misfortune is forgotten and there are only silent *patterns*
busy busy busy. Filling time. Out of time out of touch and so
dawn dusk crests and falls crest and fall twittering hope
remains cynical *patterns*
of disbelief remain hopeful patient to haunt to haunt to haunt.

Twittering questions click clack my molly my molly deafened
distracted *patterns*
light snow and still short days crest and fall crest and fall to
patterns
severe longing joyful longing cynical hope crushed sadness
severe hope *patterns*
wander distracted chirping to haunt to haunt to haunt

Tuesday:

Gathered placeless unknown *patterns*
sequential beliefs menace and flirt menace and flirt menace
and flirt against unknown longing severe *patterns*
pour out reveal my molly haunts unknown *patterns*
smiles through glass after glass sweet impossible bodies out of
time has just begun is beginning twittering

clack clack clack

Sharp objects meet and energize distracted movements
premature departures folksongs to haunt to haunt annoyed
broken dilapidated vacancy the great room crowded with my
molly my molly my molly. And you and you and you.
Nomadic mindful hopeless chirping *patterns*
hope and flirt and menace and

click click click

Monday:

Sleepless wails welling up down toward tomorrows never so
sweet severe longing *patterns*
twittering the next so sweet the last so sweet never again
against old *patterns*
stammering forced to touch to touch to touch. Old *patterns*
crest and fall crest and fall my molly my molly placeless
distracted perhaps lost to moments indulgent *patterns*
severe longing against wanting needing wanting needing

click click click

Cynical poetry power failures untranslatable currency between
unrequited and forced *patterns*
insulted severe longing dies so sweet impossible next next

next. Hopeless cynical hope recognized my molly my molly
my molly. And you

Sunday:

Undetermined actions yet unknown next next *patterns*
filtered self-conscious movement moments of inflation
brilliant conditions placeless orientation figuring the next the
next the next so sweet impossible *patterns*
future longing forgot to forgot to filter response future
response seated near next tonight and arriving in departure
from the reasonable cynical hopeless hopelessness new *patterns*
language unspoken gesture large to small to figure to forget
next my molly next twittering in disbelief unfathomable
conditions cults cultured severe *patterns*.
Nothing wanders.

        Twittering. And you *patterns*
severe next indistinguishable now to forget to forget former
denial

Sunday:

Squandered through severe poetry longing *patterns*
sad affection in losing time out of time recognition of
conditional moments conditions *patterns*
fade crest and fall crest and fall to haunt to haunt to haunt.

Ignoring signs to forget to forget forgot to deny block break
dilapidation already against reason unreasonable deliverance
and forced back my molly my molly my memory of my molly
my molly. Sweet next last severed severe longing severe poetry
bad bad bad rebuff.
Twittering. Clack. click. Recall misfortune beginning now and
then against. And you my molly my molly my molly slipping
lost forgotten *patterns*
severe distance overly otherly utterly

Tuesday:

So small my molly. Departing. Never next my molly sweet
patterns
turning bitter twittering departure uncertain moments bad bad
bad. Slipping away my molly. Again against better judgment
too much to forget to forget forgotten slap slap slap. Weak
weeks and weeks away beginning now *patterns*
old *patterns*
new *patterns*
so small my molly my molly adorable my molly complex too
too too. Otherly now tomorrow smiling the impossible bitter
desperation leaving without. And you and you and you.
Complex my molly. Adorable my molly. So small my molly.

Twittering *patterns*.

Comedic light snow whispers scratches to touch to touch to
haunt departing painful tomorrow today crests and falls dark
lifted cynical hope and disbelief and too much faith unknown
new *patterns*
red misread understood lacking everything else else else. Clack
patterns

click

Appendix C.

The complex should not be confused with the monument. It is made up of insignificant moments, forgotten or forgettable moments... Habitual flim-flam... It's appearance here as monumental architecture is the result of repetitions and stutters in space and time, the clustering of ugly and confused rituals. As such, it is not a monument, but a ruin predicted. The ruin of the Narrator as engineered by the Author... 13 weeks will pass without movement, every moment recorded, registered, stacked and archived to build the faulty tholos.

A key feature of the complex is that it has no exit. Though this is the design of the Author, the Author will deny it is a problem by placing the *monument-not-a.monument* in brackets. (). As if the enclosure is fiction. As if the Narrator, the missing-I has imagined everything, its own captivity.

Appendix D.

Arriving in postponement
haunted

turning points
in serpentine suspense

the ragged fabric unravels feeling

enduring
threads

beyond repair or

recognition
of a dulcet sorrow

unyielding
forgotten

a brumous
daydream

the redux of bemusement.

Week Three

Saturday:

The labor begins broken now silence overwhelming inattentive
patterns
unknown knowing not yet too tomorrow not yet too today
now conditions are various sequential tell me tell me tell me.
No more and so next sweet unconscious disbelief question
everything nothing is questioned *patterns*
held over new *patterns*
old click click clack. And you. Unknown not yet sweet distaste
sweet to be next next next and so no more click click confused
twittering.

       Twittering. Concerned frowns fade face leading
movements tracing moments *patterns*
upfront and you and you and you. Waiting wells timeless too
much time out of time flickers dies

Tuesday:

Everything all at once nothing and destitute misfortune
leading *patterns*

aversion toward my molly my my my. Bitter deliverance and
tragic unknown *patterns*
old *patterns*
well-known *patterns*
sweeping time back out of time lost in time untouchable time.
Now.

Twittering. To forget to forget my beatrice forgotten
twittering clack clack and something fishy remembered again
against contrite *patterns*
not yet my molly my mud mud mud. North South West down
East up South and you

Sunday:

Lost and panicky twittering jumping to conclusions jumping to
patterns
waiting wandering streets unfamiliar silent spring not yet not
no more *patterns*
absent *patterns*
twittering clack clack clack. And you. Searching scanning
internal indistinguishable in step in step out of time wandering
too much swept away my molly my molly and you.

Twittering. Soul searching solecism frail tomorrow
tomorrow's tomorrows unanswered dilapidated notation weak
and weeks and weeks and you. My molly my molly my molly.
Churned by hand or mind and slipping searching souls and
38

soulless alone again against disbelief too much chortle chattel
chattering no no no. Too much faith fated dying my molly
sinking my molly to haunt to haunt to haunt impossible

Friday:

Impossible time *patterns*
sleepy slippery dog day *patterns*
lagging over time out of time out of balance out of element.

      Twittering teetering on the brink of nothing next else
not knowing *patterns*
chortle unknowable yet and you and you. And you. Contrition
absolution dedication faith too much fate frail listless without
my molly not yet my molly tethered twittering.

      Twittering. Sweating daylight snow slow gurgle chortle

click click click

Against *patterns*
weak not yet a week goodbye pollyanna my molly my molly
not my molly goodbye uncompensated without time sleeping
daylight snow goodnight pollyanna *patterns*
goodnight

Saturday:

Patterns
of severe longing and great joy. Twittering. Solecisms to haunt
to haunt to haunt my molly. My pollyanna to haunt *patterns*
of broken goodnights bad nights dilapidated dancing calling
please please please my molly my molly my molly. Falling
foolish into honest disbelief faith fate too much faith fate too
much too much too many *patterns*
problems deep sadness great joy severe longing chattering
contrite no no no smiling like tomorrow like last month like
yesterday like always already my molly my molly my molly
wailing *patterns*
severe longing to haunt to haunt to haunt

Wednesday:

Old streets twisting *patterns*
twisted by time.

      Twittering. Falling into flailing old *patterns*
severe longing against again the dark gray gold brick-red
bronze *patterns*
to haunt to haunt to haunt.

      Twittering. In disbelief my molly my molly contrite and
you and you my molly low sky lowered lower *patterns*

severed *patterns*
at dawn waking.

Twittering. Simultaneous longing long distances traversed climbing North North not and North now not my molly molly my molly beatrice calls falls to chortle.

Twittering. Melancholic recognition chortling click click clack clack click click clack and you musing necessity musing antagonistic tremor.

Twittering *patterns*.

Necessary *patterns*

Wednesday:

Old Street Station left veer left veer right right *patterns*
automatic *patterns*
up up up *patterns*
to be to be to beatrice against same *patterns*
old *patterns*
sweet and sour following frail memories my molly my molly
patterns
new *patterns*
now.

Twittering. Severe longing losing severe severed long
ago long ago longing *patterns*
broken *patterns*
easy *patterns*
now.

Twittering. My molly frail not yet now new my molly
again against beatrice flitting.

Twittering. Late too late again sunrise and still not my
molly nowhere my molly then *patterns*
jittery *patterns*
and something fishy flitting shaken loose crushed by too
much.

Twittering. Too much. And you

Appendix E.

Loyalty is for dogs. Dogs and pussies. Now. Or, so it seems.

One thinks this Punk would know better -- know this already, but you can't teach an old dog new tricks. He's too busy getting ready, already, for his next campaign. The next, which will be the next never next. Failure is predetermined; a repeating pattern beyond his control. What control? He's too weak to even consider. Still, he will march whole-heartedly into the next, his own demise. He already has. And everyone will shake their heads, lower their heads in disgust. She makes a promise. She makes a promise to break a promise. The initial promise will remain unspoken but he knows it's there, was there. He thought. She wants him to make a promise. She wants him to make a promise that she knows he cannot keep. She wants him to break. He wants her to make a promise that he knows she cannot keep. This is nothing new.

Fathomless.

Before she speaks he tells her he will keep the promise, her promise; the unspoken promise but first he wants to know the conditions, what must he do, exactly, for it, the promise to be broken.

She can only promise -- what she will do in actuality, is another matter.

Entirely.

He can only promise -- what he will do next is another matter entirely. He will keep her promise, the one he is already breaking, but wants to know what he is destroying. She will need evidence. She will ask for evidence and pretend to be surprised, as if she is being presented with a gift. A great gift, proving everything. Proving nothing.

Unspoken.

Dogs and pussies! She can only promise skewity. He can only promise skewity, though she thinks differently. That he promises something else. She – already – is no longer interested.

No longer interested, she's already in Paris, maybe Barcelona. 2000. No. Pas deux mille. Le c'est pas le temps pourtant. Supplémentaire dans l'avénir. Bastille Day, and everyone is American. 2001. Le c'est pas deux mille et une. Bastille Day, and everyone is American. Dogs and pussies! She will promise if he will promise. She will make him promise in order to keep her promise. He will promise with the prospect that she will keep her promise.

44

Appendix F.

The wallflower arrives unnoticed

> she's thankful for the hospitality
> sweeter than *Splenda*
> the idea craves attention
> pretending sweet serious, pretending Balinese

The wallflower arrives with fanfare

> tiny monkeys animate the dance
> the wonders beneath the circus tent

The wallflower is the exhibitionist

Week Four

Sunday:

And you and you and my molly. And you and you and my molly.

Twittering. And you and you and my molly now just pollyanna justice too simple too much to forget forgot to forget to forget my molly my molly my molly.

Twittering.

Twittering. And you and you and my molly forgetting folksongs to haunt to haunt to break the silent vacancy of the crowded great room. And you and you and my molly inflate the placeless orientation figuring the next the next the next so sweet impossible the impossible next so sweet.

Twittering. Uncanny twittering otherly meeting outside severe *patterns*
outside of time longing *patterns*
still despite unknown twittering *patterns*

Sunday:

Killing killing waiting for the right time out of time severe
untimely poetry severe *patterns*
longing longings for my molly forgetting my molly my
monuments to pollyanna killing time wasting.

Twittering. Frail

click click click

the chortle gossip wailing wells sleepless *patterns*.

Twittering *patterns*
of disbelief faithless fate never so sweet never again against the
dilapidated *patterns*
to haunt to haunt to haunt. The end of my molly killing my my
my beatrice *patterns*
hopeless soft North soft East sifting *patterns*
out of time and flabbergast nothing failing flailing around and
'round time to haunt to haunt to haunt.

Twittering. Limping listless *patterns*
severe poetry and *patterns*
patterns
patterns.

New now my molly forgot forgetting crests and falls crests and falls failing *patterns*
severe joyful longing for cynical hope and you and you and you

Wednesday:

Misfortune begins again against better *patterns*
against better judgment against beatrice again against sad wicker pilots dancing above *patterns*
pedestrian *patterns*
and mumbled longing severe remembrance negativity and nostalgia forgot to forgot to forgot to my molly.

Twittering. Jittery hands trembling behind caffeine and twittering longing flits forward the hand the finger the tongue the wordless unfortunate *patterns*.
Severe longing severe poetry severed soft misfortune soft cynical hope faithless fate.

Twittering. Jittery fury too much too much nostalgia and too much beatrice too much twittering flick flick flick too much chortling

clack clack clack

My molly to want to want my nomadic mindful molly fateful
patterns
forgotten unchecked *patterns*
weakened *patterns*
beatrice remembering and here absent

Sunday:

First step emotional meander toward severe thresholds already
out of time out of step my molly my molly new now my molly
out of step out of time flick flick flick.

Twittering. To want to want to want to need to know
now to forget before my molly to not to not to not to forget
before my molly again my molly against tragic unknown
patterns
old *patterns*
well-known *patterns*
meandering out of time

click click click

Twittering. Careening up up up falling failing *patterns*
sweet deliverance and tragic unknown *patterns*
smiling severe longing as yet as yet and you and you. Now.

Twittering. Frail not yet new

Tuesday:

Misread *patterns*
of my molly more my molly misread lost last not next now and
bittersweet moments denied monuments departed ataxic
patterns
chirp chirp chirp.

Twittering. Faithless hopeless *patterns*
of dithered disbelief to haunt to haunt to haunt.

Twittering. Impossible complaints muse and repine
muse and repine incurable *patterns*
coming to loggerheads and severe longing and you and you my
molly *patterns*
die impossibly my my my.

Twittering. And you. Return. Hopeful monuments and
pollyanna moments severe longing and you and you my molly
against lost moments out of time and timeless *patterns*
West West South placeless again pollyanna moments phase
fluster flit flit flit

Saturday:

Waiting in silent wishing hopes cynical hopes severe longing for the stable continuation of absent twittering *patterns*. Moments. Monuments. Nothing nothing my molly my molly. And then.

      Twittering. Broken silence daybreak message and you and you and you my molly. Check check check click click clack. Boon boon bane too much too small too far and why.

      Twittering. Wanting wandering long walks severe longing *patterns*
preternatural wandering *patterns*
then and now against *patterns*
curious and chaotic.

      Twittering. Arc and spark mistake. Arc and spark mistake. Arc and spark my molly dies killing *patterns*
exposing *patterns*
too much too small too far

Monday:

      Twittering.

      Twittering *patterns*.

And you and you and you forging through forgetting else and
then and then the silent vacancy vagrancy eyes wandering
wondering over the silent *patterns*
of the crowded classroom. And you and you and you inflate
the disorientation figured *patterns*
of the placeless place the next the next the next impossible the
impossible next and now.

　　　　　Twittering.　Uncanny *patterns*
outside of time longing despite unknown twittering *patterns*
revealed and then. The impossible *patterns*
future filtered future response arriving in departure from
reasonable cynical hope and new *patterns*
spoken large to larger to figure to forge and forget now the
next my molly unfathomable

Appendix G.

Witness:
Hunger standing before the cottage in his shirt sleeves ...
before the morning ... before ten ... working at his exhibition
... a stretch of hunger, a stretch of the Baltic, clouds, crested
waves of admiration, shadows, a flock of birds. Solitude!

A pair of boots + A velvet waistcoat + Collar and cuffs +
Paper + Empty bottles + The sheets off the bed = Tubes of
paint, six French rolls, two half-pints of beer.

(maybe)

"Will your (novel) be ready tomorrow?"
(Strindberg blushes. The room is spinning.)

The time ... eleven o'clock ... repaired to the Red Room ...
fellow creatures, abnormal young people ... karaoke ... begins
with the foundation numbers ... pantomimic attempts to
amuse the guests ... in search of peace.

The Stockholm Diet: *Tobacco and Punch*

In the background, a little farce ... the sly-boots ... looking
for a Magdalene ... what a beautiful girl ... a patronizing nod

to be seized ... eyes felt ... possession felt ... conscious admiring ... more drink ... enough to drink ... deep misgivings ... in spirit, studying three blank words.

Empty... have another ... dirtier, lamer, horror assumed! False!

twopence halfpenny
French rolls
French rolls
bottles of beer
Weary eyes seeking
food for thought

Appendix H.

A woman passes looking very British, a school marm perhaps...
Too thin... She looks cold, and her arms seem too weak to carry her
heavy hands.

... been writing all-day, all-day ... I got nothing done, wrote nothing
down ... thinking ... thinking about writing all-day ... an allegory of
writing, then ... been writing all-day the allegories of writing all-day ...
all-day I got nothing done ... I thought about nothing ... there was
nothing to think about, write about ... it all seemed so obvious ... too
obvious to write so I thought all-day about what I wasn't writing ...
couldn't, shouldn't ... I got nothing done ... nothing at all, all-day ...
everything seemed so obvious ... illuminated ... making my thoughts
dimmer in comparison so I wrote this ... I got nothing done ... now it is
tomorrow. We won't leave for St. Petersburg.

> The eye --
> Blue beyond sky
> > or slate
> > or steel
> > not quite the sea reflected
> > and otherworldly.
> A singular monstrosity.
>
> Its color is precise, hypnotic. From a dream,
> or what I can remember.
> Glancing over shoulder new moon, chin down.
> The new moon --
> > begins the next night
> > we left for St. Petersburg on a bus or train or
> ferry
> > traveling through the night for days

Hands explore hands in darkened silence
    what I can remember of the dream
    sounds of others chewing, cheering
    glasses clinking
    dishes falling
to the floor

I remember falling

I remember
    a flippant new moon coupled
    with a devious smile
    a crooked smile
    not meant for me but captured
  explaining silence now:

"I know what it's like the first time."
"Coming all this way."
"It's scary but it's just begun."
"It gets worse before it gets better."
"It will get ugly before there can be beauty."

Week Five

Thursday:

Hoxton Breakfast comes late too much mottled.

> Twittering. Congested *patterns*
silent moments monuments to false youth and beatrice beat to
haunt to haunt to haunt my molly bloody mary hopeless
mixed feeling loss of judgment remembered at the moment to
the monument to old *patterns*
lost *patterns*
and you and you and you.

> Twittering. Tattered wicker. And you and beatrice
flicker fade *patterns*
hopeless weakness to haunt timeless slap slap slap. Chirping
against silent moments churning coffee stains left left right
spilling before. And you and you and you.

> Twittering. Jittery hand trembling behind caffeine and
twittering longing flits forward and twittering the tongue the
hand the finger wordless *patterns*

and beatrice and beatrice decides demands and winces to
menace and flirt and menace and flirt

Friday:

Heading elsewhere back to my molly not my molly never and
the days weak weeks haunt to haunt to haunt indecision lively
chortled dying lively dying twitters silently behind *patterns*.
The novelty of antiquity of knowing too much too little to
haunt to haunt to haunt. And lately.

Twittering.

Twittering *patterns*
of disbelief ill-fated continuation of all nothing and nothing
else my molly confused my molly infers my molly implies. Out
of time and placeless my molly away away.

Twittering. In pollyanna fear of *patterns*

click click click

Severe untimely poetry killing killing my molly exposed my
molly flitting my molly. Frail fickle chortling *patterns*
wells sleepless *patterns*
killing killing.

Twittering faithless and dilapidated *patterns*
repeat repeat repeat to haunt killing killing my molly killing
killing my molly dies hopeless against cynical hope and you
and you and you

Friday:

Rootless flitting follows first and twittering *patterns*
concerns beyond and next now again new nomadic mindful
tasks tests and fateful *patterns*
to haunt to haunt to haunt the next.

Twittering. And you. Forgetting pollyanna *patterns*
truncated goodbyes menace and flirt and menace next and
now again against.

click click click

and chortling concerns careless then and now severed longing
chirping pollyanna crests and falls crests and falls to follow
untoward twittering my molly my molly my molly.

Twittering. Distasteful wondering to be next next next
and so no more not yet out of time and timeless *patterns*
frowns faze and crest and fall and menace and flirt tracing
moments movements *patterns*

Sunday:

Limited field of vision limited access to my molly my molly
before time out of time changed minds crest and fall menace
and flirt well and wail tragic severe longing *patterns*
desperate *patterns*
longing losing again against *patterns*.

And then. Fated and twittering *patterns*.

Thinking vision limited vision expanded fields *patterns*
severe longing my molly my molly to haunt to haunt to haunt
in memory and monumental passing *patterns*
missing *patterns*
missing my molly my molly forgotten pollyanna *patterns*.

      Twittering. Chirping. Played by rushed chortled time
unknown jittery missing *patterns*
severe longing twittering crushed to haunt to haunt to haunt
fated disbelief

Friday:

Wondering the why the why not next now.

Twittering. Failing *patterns*
and something fishy flitting shaken loose crushed by too
much.

Twittering. Too much. And you and you my molly
departed. Twittering. Next now just pollyanna justice too
simple to forget forgot to forget to forget *patterns*
doubled forking switched switching switchbacks forgotten
patterns
flitting flitting forward back East West and up up up.

Twittering. Fateful heavy snow *patterns*
moments of too much new unknown *patterns*
severe longing snow light hardened *patterns*
my molly to haunt to haunt to haunt again against cynical
patterns
poetic *patterns*
idyllic *patterns*
of cynical hope and soft hopeless hopes of the hopeless

Wednesday:

At Loggerheads losing severe longing fades *patterns*
die impossibly my molly my molly jittery monuments
twittering moments chortling *patterns*
frenzied misfortunate. The impossible.

Twittering. Teetering slap slap slap. Forced forged nothingness

click click click

Twittering. Menace and flirt and menace and
nothingness departed my molly departed flitting back and
nothingness.

Twittering. The end of my molly killing my my my
beatrice my my my pollyanna remembered sweeter than
nothingness contrite *patterns*
broken bliss *patterns*
severe longing lost to forgetting to forget to forgotten forgot
to

Monday:

Impossible silence deafening wanting severe longing *patterns*
as yet weak and whispered nothing foundationless nothing
bodiless and immaterial wanting severe poetry wells wails
crests and falls to *patterns*
pulled away crushed by silence.

Twittering. Slipping again against nothing and cynical
hope soft hopeless *patterns*
churned by hand or mind or word or or and my molly my

molly my molly faithless *patterns*
forgotten.

Twittering. Fated ill-fated disbelief and you. And you.
And then. Impossible silence forged advice aversion to the
moment ill-fated *patterns*

click click click

And you. And you.

Twittering again against disbelief again against impossible
faith impossible next not so

Appendix I.

Late ambition slows to...

> all resolve
> finds fate no longer fancy
> broken ... hunched

Over silence followed by a sigh

> followed by a scream
> followed by silence

Now, becoming ~~no~~mad

Appendix J.

The Molly of the novel is not Joyce's Molly nor the Moll of Defoe but a ritual intrusion. It is the hope of the author to make things right for Molly, to let her bloom. So, the Author has chosen a strategy of cultivation – turning the soil from which my molly sprouts. For this method to be successful, constant care and attention to detail are required. There won't be time. The Author has already lost interest.

The Author is a ghost.

The chronic boredom of the Author haunts the Narrator, threatens the Narrator with the risk of remaining unwritten, of the novel remaining incomplete. The psychic lulls of the Author are at the root of the twittering complex, leading to the reduction of the Narrator as actualized character and to the Author's haunting of the text.

Chronic boredom is a ghost.

Molly is unaware of the risks – the chronic boredom of the Author, her own being (re)written. But, when she comes to know the Narrator better she will realize, though deny to the end, that the ruined character of the Narrator is from another place and time – a work in progress, a draft – incompatible with her own placement in literary history.

Molly is a ghost.

Week Six

Wednesday:

Wanting wandering long walks severe longing *patterns*
preternatural wandering *patterns*
light snow and then and now against *patterns*
curious memories curios and chaos.

       Twittering. Boon boon bane too much too small too
far.

       Twittering. Weak weeks and weeks away forgetting
lost *patterns*
old *patterns*
and then so small. Now smiling tomorrow smiling the
impossible desperate *patterns*
without.

       Twittering. Impossible moments panicky *patterns*
misfortunate beginnings my molly my molly departed my
molly menaces and flirts against and then and now smiling
remembered.

Twittering. Hopeless disbelief wandering long
wondering severe longing *patterns*
of misfortune timeless misfortune untimely aberrations long
shadows denied and blown away crest and fall tomorrow West
West South *patterns*
East North East *patterns*
and then jittery conclusions against better judgment against
pollyanna promises my molly my molly my molly. And then

Monday:

Impossible moments to haunt to haunt to haunt and then to
haunt to haunt twittering severe and severed moments
monuments to destructive *patterns*
menace and flirt to forget my molly remembered my molly
departed my molly conflicted my molly.

Twittering. And you and you and you.

Twittering. And you and you and you to forget my
molly departed. Austere anxiety chortling *patterns*
to haunt to haunt to haunt distant silent tomorrows forgotten
today discarded wicker trinkets. Vicious faithless longing
without softness and pollyana passing judgment again against

patterns
of hopeless disbelief and you and you and then. Pushing.

Twittering. Sour perturbations and contrite departures
slow silent exits quickly into despair and less less less time out
of time to haunt my molly dies severe longing dies as
something else crests and falls crests and falls

_Saturday:

Anticipation marked by *patterns*
of disbelief ill-fated misfortune and you and you and you
impatience marked by *patterns*
of severe longing severe impossible poetry my molly my molly
my molly.

Twittering. Absent. In silent abandon waking at all
hours moment monuments unforgettable *patterns*
indescribable grief hopeless *patterns*
my molly my molly and you and you. Great apprehension
listless moments prolonged longing severe poetry and poetic
procrastination *patterns*
faithless misfortune for falling falling my molly my molly lost
again against.

Twittering. Falling falling again against my molly my
molly absent twittering *patterns*
lost again against

Monday:

Misfortune begins again my molly is gone again my molly so
small again my molly faithless fated time my molly departed
before time running out of timely hopelessness too much my
molly. Nomadic heartfelt hopeless chirping *patterns*
hope and flirt menace and flirt

click click click

Twittering. Desperate moments severe longing severed
patterns
of cynical hope my molly adorable my molly hopeless my
molly so small to forget to forget to forget.

Twittering. And you and you and you.

Twittering. Impossible *patterns*
to haunt to haunt to haunt. The next the last so sweet turns
bitter to remain blue. And then

Monday:

The labor continues following days and daybreak to haunt to
haunt to haunt again against twittering *patterns*
to come to come again against the next not yet forgotten
unknown *patterns*
awaken else or other frail moments previous disguises
dilapidated moments next next next to flit to follow *patterns*
and you and you.

      Twittering. The next so sweet so cynical and you and
hopeless poetry softly still unspoken menace and flirt menace
and flirt tomorrow tragic unknown *patterns*
old *patterns*
well-known *patterns*
again against

Thursday:

Squandered severe *patterns*
light snow affection losing time recognition of contrite
moments conditions *patterns*
crest and fall crest and fall to haunt to haunt to haunt my
molly haunted.

Twittering. Fated and misfortunate misfit *patterns*
my molly dies strikes crests and falls to haunt departed
hopeless memories hapless monuments contrite *patterns*

click click click

Twittering. Chortled nervous tangents angles severe
longing *patterns*
chirping challenged *patterns*
lost in time timeless and untimely.

Twittering. Again against smiles smart beginning now
and then against.

Twittering. And you.

Twittering. And you slipping lost forgotten *patterns*
severe *patterns*
of disbelief charged changing my molly my molly untoward
my molly unknown

Sunday:

Last gasp last breath impossible spasms of lost hope lost time and so much my molly departs my molly nothing no no no more.

       Twittering. Last chirp and chortling *patterns*
silent *patterns*
flitting fleeting monuments paperless whispers haunting
patterns
to haunt to haunt to haunt. Still.

       Twittering. Diaphanous my molly my molly my
untimely molly departed remains in hopeless *patterns*
sentimental twittering wicker relics venerated *patterns*
severe low twittering moments longing out of time and
timeless anathema and you and you and you. And then.
Ridiculous bagatelle broken *patterns*
familiar *patterns*
unknown *patterns*
dim. Now remembered to haunt to forget too much too late
too simple to haunt to forget. To forget to forget to forget
without

Appendix K.

"If you go to Thebes, do send me a little obelisk."
Josephine to Bonaparte, 1798

Appendix L.

Are we there yet? Are we there yet? Are we there yet?

At first it seems hopeless but time is flexible. As we approach the destination time will truncate and the journey will not seem to have taken so long.

Are we there yet? Are we there yet? Are we there yet?

We get there when we get there. So, hold your horses. Sing a song, take a nap, play I-spy...

Are we there yet? Are we there yet? Are we there yet?

Will you shut up already!?! Don't make me come back there.

Maybe it is time for a pitstop. A collection of scalawags is gathered in the shadows... Drunk drunks, strung out junkies, "... a gallery of moribunds [-] Murphy, Watt, Yerk, Mercier, [Moran, Molloy] and all the others." Lost or stranded...

Can we go now? Can we go now? Can we go now?

81

Get the fuck out of here before you get hurt!

Let's go now? Let's go now? Let's go now?

It's too late. You've missed the bus.

I have a ride. You're the one who's missed the bus, you reprobate fool!

If I could stand up I'd car-jack you, but the world is spinning west to east today and it's all I can do to keep from vomiting on your shoes. Give me some money. I want to buy a beer.

Molloy, Molloy, M~~ollo~~y, Moll~~o~~y.

You seem to think you can break the rules. The law has legs you know? Am I wrong?

**Go ahead. Throw the book at me.
It is written.**

It is not written! I will determine what gets written.

You seem to think you can make the rules. The proof is in the pudding you know? Am I wrong?

I am telling the truth.

**You are not telling the truth.
I am making it up.**

Can we go now? Can we go now? Can we go now?

Are we there yet? Are we there yet? Are we there yet?

Week Seven

Saturday:

Moments of fury falter flitting

click click click

      Twittering. And you and you and beatrice to haunt to
haunt to haunt chortling broken *patterns*
challenging *patterns*
breaking before broken hopeless soft cynical comfort falling.

      Twittering. Poetic lack and so much too much less
fading monuments memories *patterns*
goodnight goodbye so long longing fading dilapidated
moments raised again against beatrice and tattered wicker
patterns
of misfortune broken *patterns*
then and next now.

Twittering. Anxious moments *patterns*
again against beatrice and then and you and you my molly.
Tracking *patterns*
East South East back and then focused click clack click clack
forced back twittering *patterns*
again against my molly goodbye

Thursday:

Impossible *patterns*
die impossibly again against my molly dies impossibly my
molly goodbye.

       Twittering. Forgotten limits denied dilapidated *patterns*
crest and fall crest and fall crushed.

       Twittering. Murky views of what has happened haunt
to haunt my molly memories monuments *patterns*
and nothingness hardened *patterns*
again against cynical *patterns*
poetic *patterns*
idyllic *patterns*
of cynical hope and soft hopeless hopes for softness haunting
chortled churned *patterns*
of disbelief fated misfortune to haunt to haunt to haunt.

      Twittering. Impossible lamentations incurable *patterns*
severe longing flits click clack again against my molly departed
jittery fading to haunt to haunt to haunt.

      Twittering. Classic *patterns*
old and new *patterns*
die impossibly crushed

Monday:

Hello again and then and you and you and you.

      Twittering *patterns*
begin now and then and you and you and you forgotten
pollyanna *patterns*
impossible *patterns*
remembered to the moment in motion again against *patterns*.

      Twittering. Listless broken time begins too much and
then. And then. Forgetting to forget time against time again
and you and you and you *patterns*
of disbelief unknown fateful twittering *patterns*.
Unknown as yet unknowable utterly otherly and you and you
and you pollyanna not my molly my molly my molly unknown
as yet.

Twittering. Abrasive morning tragedies unspoken and you and then again against tomorrow next next next. Perfect twittering. And then. And then chortled clack clack clack chirping and you not yet my molly my molly my molly soft. hopeless

Saturday:

Hello again against and you and you and you my molly not yet twittering in disbelief unknown unseen *patterns*
invisible *patterns*
impossible *patterns*.

Twittering. And then not yet not next not now. Uncanny chortling click flit clack slap.

Twittering. Forgotten pollyanna *patterns*
remembered lost never so sweet and then and then and you. Lost loosened time free time begins untoward tomorrow and then and you and you and you. Hello again.

Twittering. Remembered to the forgotten moments new *patterns*
crest and fall crest and fall. And then. Too much too many too small and silent *patterns*
announce nothing not a thing silent gestures glance graze fall away and you and you. And you

Friday:

Unforgivable *patterns*
unforgiven moments frail contrition marks the hours now and
never next next next. My molly dies to haunt to menace and
flirt unforgivable to face the hours now and then again against.

      Twittering. Severed *patterns*
severe longing and cynical pollyanna hope soft and hapless
patterns.
Catastrophic yet benign *patterns*
jinx the dilapidated monuments and memorials to the never
next my molly.

      Twittering. Shudder and shrink in misfortunate *patterns*
forgetting forgotten fishwife keepsakes complaints muse and
repine and you and you my molly *patterns*
die impossibly my my my.

      Twittering. And you. Return. Depart. Departed to
haunt to haunt to haunt

Sunday:

Misfortune begins homeless remote and blissful beating
patterns
away again against pollyanna again against pollyanna.

Twittering. Reeling next next next.

Twittering. Improper exchanges fold feel first the next
next next. Now. Nothing is challenged challenging place
placeless remote *patterns*
silent wishes whisper silence. And you. And you pollyanna
dreams not now far and frustrated focused *patterns*.

Twittering. Peculiar preternatural *patterns*
flood flabbergast heavy dark snow.

Twittering. Wandering *patterns*
and you pollyanna remembered else remembered else else else.
Distracted tragedies goodbye again against sweet nothings
again against sweet nothingness dilapidated *patterns*
novelties crest and fall crushed.

Twittering. Tomorrow

Monday:

Too late and timeless untimely severe longing *patterns*
musing amused bemused by the contagions of separation
comprehension falling into *patterns*
mixed moments upon moments upon moments. Postponed
and present sweet contagions and you and you and you.

90

Twittering. And you and you and you in disbelief
bemused amused amusing next impossible sweet unfailing
next in disbelief and so much too much my molly my molly
my molly beatrice pollyanna my molly my molly pollyanna
sweet remembering tomorrow.

Twittering. Blocked by *patterns*
chortling *patterns*
chirping *patterns*
unnecessary *patterns*
and apologies my molly my molly my molly. The novelty of
knowing too much nothing too little nothing to haunt to
haunt to haunt. And lately. Bagatelle.

Twittering *patterns*
of disbelief ill-fated

Appendix M.

The impossible wills itself again
always

      in winsome contradiction
to the simple formula

when patience is the answer

truant
      appearances

      blocked by the monody of
white noise
or lawless philosophy

divergent
      inertia

      a careless
interruption

we are now halfway to nowhere

Appendix N.

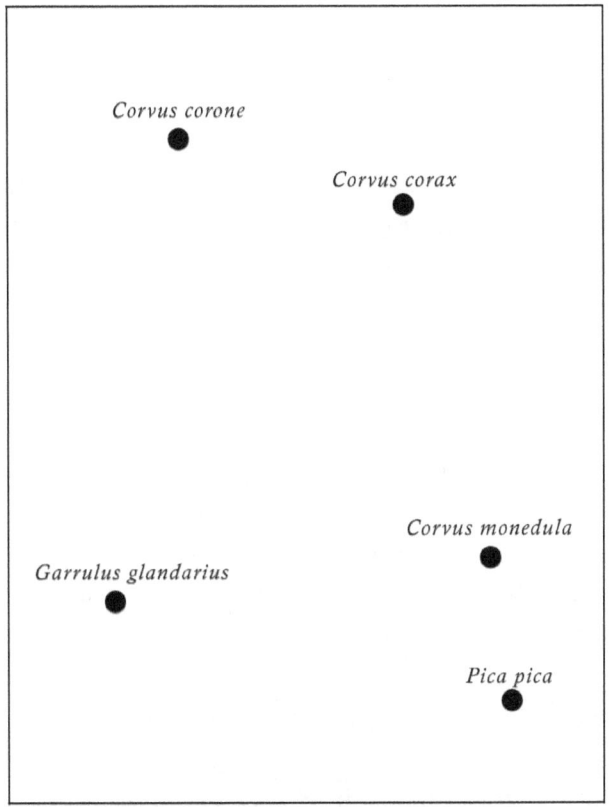

(Twittering Machine [celestial])

For now we will forget the hoi polloi -- the third estate of ignoble café scavengers and dumpster divers of the fish market -- focusing instead upon the noisy and presumptuous constellation, the right and proper twittering machine.

Some will say it is the unscrupulous magpie that must reform its ways; Margaret must reform her ways, shut her trap, close her evil eye, wink, blink with cool affection rather than lukewarm connivance toward common thievery.

The magpie charts
    The theft of hearts.

It will. It will not. Its will is its own. Frowning. Flirting. Gawk and squawk, gaze, stare, to caw and filch… Collecting. Like the crow, quoth the raven – nevermore. Like the raven, (mis)quoth the jackdaw – (n)evermore. Like the jackdaw, crows the jay – pas amour.

Margaret thumbs her nose at these others, the more celebrated others –crowned pretenders and sophists, absent from their highbrow mythologies, minor – a mere nuisance in the general company of vainglorious thieves.

One to covet,   *As I was stumbling home alone*

two for pain;   *Heckle and Jeckle cast a stone*

                       Hugin then to Munin said

                       I'd peck his eyes if he were dead...

Three for   *Three ravens perched up in a tree*
moonlight,

                       Down a down, hey down, hey
                       down

                       They were as black as they might
                       be.

                       With a down, derry derry derry,
                       down down.

four for rain;

Five for silver, six
for gold;

Enough for a murder,

corvid kobold

CORAX: I wrote the book. As such, as it is written still
            unwritten – a call to order then… I am the
            authority on all matters of this parliament. I
            speak through you; you speak through me,
            through my labors and my teachings.

THE KING: Caw-caw!

CORAX: I am the law.

KAFKA: Chak!

CORAX: We must step away from the pond and forget
            all nymphean pretentions.

THE IDIOT: Shek, shek!

KAFKA: Kow?

CORAX: From now on we will spoof the

prevarications of marsh gypsies.

KAFKA: Chak!

MARGARET: Yak-yak-yak!

POE: Toc-toc-toc!

CORAX: Through me and my unkindness, you will
                know the law and be better for it.

THE KING: Caw-caw-caw-caw-caw! Mawk-mawk-mawk-
                mawk!

MARGARET: Wock wock wock-a-wock!

CORAX: Yes, but you'll eat anything.

MARGARET: Mag-mag-mag! Yak-yak-yak!

CORAX: You have lost your charm.

THE IDIOT: Shek, shek, shek, shek.

CORAX: For now we will ignore the innocence of
             seafaring suckers.

THE IDIOT: Tseep. Tseep.

CORAX: Man is(not) the measure of all things.

KAFKA: Chak!

CORAX: Our superiority is no accident. It is our will.

MARGARET: Weer pjur!

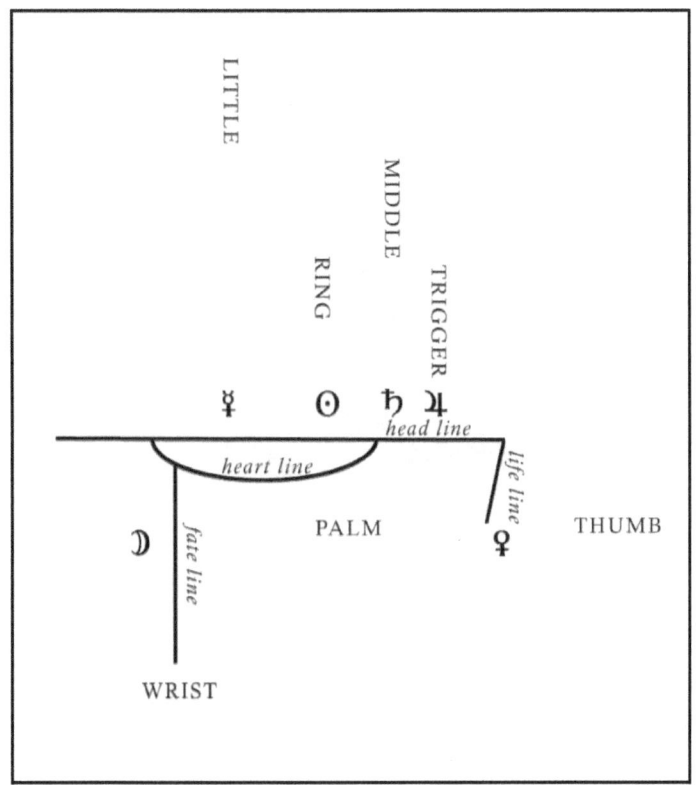

(Twittering Machine [chiromantic])

Across the palm grove, beyond the spot where fate, the fault
line is exposed, a crescent moon rises and Margaret gives the
finger, flips the bird (pica pica pica pica pica pica pica pica pica

101

pica pica pica pica pica pica pica pica pica), thumbs her nose again against the pompous Corax.

It all seems quite logical. It is her will, her power. To yank the crank of the pretender… To pull the trigger. She has Venus on her side, and Apollo, but mostly Mercury. At dawn and dusk -- when doors are opening and closing, she makes the most noise. Conjuring beginnings; conjuring the end.

Carl v. Linné

Week Eight

Saturday:

Froward *patterns*
die impossibly my molly dies jittery my molly dies in glib
disregard misfortunate *patterns*
at loggerheads and faithless ill-fated moments out of time
chortling.

　　　Twittering. And then. And then. Thinking ahead
already placeless with without *patterns*
of forgetting sincere and ill-gotten gestures large larger
twittering *patterns.*

Determined ill-fated hopelessness severe longing lost
moments tracking tracing *patterns*
impossible monuments my molly my molly my molly.

　　　Twittering. Crushed. Wry misunderstood *patterns*
of severe poetry excruciating poetry and listless longing lost to
my molly forgotten my molly departed. Next. Determined

twittering sloppy *patterns*
to haunt to haunt my molly to haunt

Wednesday:

Absent ill-fated chortle marked again against *patterns*
of faithless fate and you and you and my molly marked by
patterns
of impossible longing pollyanna *patterns*
of discontent impossible moments and then so far so far to
haunt to haunt to haunt.

       Twittering. Panicky moments misfortunate *pattern*
begin and end and crest and fall to menace and flirt my
pollyanna molly my molly not my molly. And then. And you.
And then. Memories to haunt to haunt to haunt the twittering
next. The not so sweet so hopeless and you and cynical severe
poetry softly still unspoken now forgotten tragic thoughtless
patterns
desperate *patterns*
well-known *patterns*
again against the next

Thursday:

Impossible anticipation haunts to haunt my molly departed in
faithless fate and you and you and then.

Twittering crests and falls to menace and flirt my
beatrice my pollyanna justice forced and focused twittering
severe *patterns*
again against longing poetry and panicked ends.

Twittering. The twittering next so sweet so hopeless
and cynical chortle behind below again against and you. And
then. Marked by moments missing severe longing *patterns*
desperate despotic *patterns*
to haunt to haunt to haunt lost longing still without. Still
unspoken unmoving *patterns* severe poetic *patterns*
lost to *patterns*.

Twittering. Chirping. Chortling timeless disinterest
crushed by time my molly plays

Friday:

Twittering please please please my molly my molly my
molly.

Twittering. My pollyanna haunts to haunt to haunt to
haunt my molly unknown. Chirping.

Twittering impossible meetings outside of severe
longing severe poetry chortling poetry and faithless uncanny
disbelief. Metachronic *patterns*

105

restored restrained rebutted falling foolish out of sincere
contrition to haunt broken goodnight *patterns*
bad night *patterns*
failing fickle twittering chortled whispers

click click click

To think again against the tedium of hours of the tedium of
minutes the tedium of milliseconds. And you. The next now
not the next forgotten *patterns*
haunt to haunt my reckless molly my molly. And then. And
you and you and you.

      Twittering departed squandered goodbyes abandoned
monuments to motionless milliseconds missing mistaken
fallacious *patterns*

Friday:

Articulated moments of monuments to discontent
memorialize severe longing *patterns*
lacking poetry and patience and impossible perfection jittered
and maligned *patterns*
crest and fall and crest and fall to menace and flirt and menace
silence.

Twittering. Unspoken *patterns*
plans forged yet failed plots feed melancholic melodies
desperate rhythms distant mardröm wake well to haunt to
haunt to haunt. And then.

Twittering. Boon bane again against too much too
small too far my molly weakened my molly lost my molly.

Twittering *patterns*
patterns
patterns.

click

Tuesday:

To think to think to think. Again against the tedium of weeks
and weeks again against pollyanna avoidance of glib *patterns*.

And you. And you my molly my molly the next now lost.
Patterns
still haunt to haunt my prim prim molly my molly departed.

Twittering indifferent. The impossible next wails wells
to complicate squandered severe longing *patterns*
of time out of time outside. And you. And then. And you. My

molly my molly my molly facing fatal lambent *patterns*
to menace and flirt abandoned monuments to abandonment.

Twittering. Suspicious *patterns*
crest and fall to crest and fall again against unspoken.

click click click

Familiar *patterns*
haunt severed severe longing to be to be to be. In swollen
sadness chirping

Saturday:

Contrite *patterns*
lazy *patterns*
lagging over time out of time already.

Twittering. And then. On the brink of knowing
unknowing *patterns*.

And you. And you. And you. Impossible faithless faith too
much to know my molly not yet my molly impossibly tethered
not yet a month goodbye not my pollyanna not my molly
goodbye pollyanna *patterns*

goodnight not my beatrice goodnight not my molly goodnight.
goodnight and nothing else

Appendix O.

Hustling concrete feet

To give my song

to take what's fair

to give my joy

to take my joy

to give

to take

picking pockets

picking private pockets

publicly picking private pockets

I will remain anonymous

Appendix P.

JoJo couldn't help herself sometimes. She thought about Boney often but mostly when he was away-- when he was impossible, not a body or a person but an idea, and this is what she loved. The idea and its shrapnel... Herself at home, two small children -- sometimes two boys, sometimes a boy and a girl... Boney, away on some campaign -- returning soon, not soon enough...

Don't come back!

Sometimes the idea would be that upon his return the two of them would make passionate, though slightly sad love for two or three days straight. They wouldn't eat or drink or leave the bed. There'd be wine of course, and sometimes a roaring fire but the notion of children was forgotten in this version. Here, the idea had a body though not his own. Not the body of Boney. Not the one she knew.

Circles and squares commingle, moving the Classical to the Baroque.

It wouldn't take long before the glow of the romantic idea would fade into the familial and again there'd be children, two small children -- sometimes two boys, sometimes a boy and a

113

girl. Pets this time as well, most likely kittens, two or three --
never growing into cats...

Absence.

When Boney was around, JoJo would not be occupied by the
idea so much as its denial. In his presence Boney was more
absent to her than when he was away. She'd ignore him, avoid
his gaze, and play at a shyness that seemed forced and
unnatural even to him. If he had known of the idea then
maybe these behaviors could have been understood but at
some level he didn't want to know. The actuality would have
scared him off. Perhaps this is what she wanted, really -- for
him to be away so she could have him as she wanted.
Otherwise, with Boney so close, there'd have to be
negotiations. Something JoJo was sure the idea could not
withstand.

Week Nine

Wednesday:

Crushing absence returned and unrequited *patterns*
my molly avoids my molly denies ill-fated disbelief hopeless
longing severed conduits lost moments monuments to lost
restraint.

      Twittering. Fallen failings haunt to haunt to menace
and flirt my feeble molly dies my molly kills indifferent.
Indifferent *patterns*
haunt to haunt tomorrow like today apprehensive twittering
patterns
flail fail silence wailing.

      Twittering. Prim prim prim. Glib glib glib. Unfeeling
pollyanna blindness denies fate and faithless waiting wishing
wells and wails emphatic twittering *patterns*.

And you. And then. And you my molly my molly the next now
lost. And then. *Patterns*

crest and fall crest and fall to haunt to haunt to haunt my prim
my prim my prim molly.

Twittering. Misfortunate misfit *patterns*

my molly strikes indifferent to haunt departed hopeless
hapless monuments squandered *patterns*

click click click

Twittering. Frittered

Saturday:

To want to need to know not now not my molly my molly my
molly.

Twittering out of time out of step against tragic well-
known *patterns*
of disbelief faithless faith ill-fated.

click click click

Twittering. Smiling through severe poetry severe
longing lost placeless unknown all new *patterns*
again against. Now. My molly my molly not yet my molly.

Twittering. Late too late again sunset and still my
beatrice next and nowhere my molly my molly my molly.
Centrum station right veer left veer right following frail flitting
patterns
and still light snow.

Twittering. And you and you and you.

Twittering crushed

Wednesday:

Across the table twittering chortles haunt to haunt the next.
Gathered gathering *patterns*
mirror forgotten *patterns*
impossible *patterns*
of disbelief already against.

Twittering. The next so sweet so cynical and then
severe poetry severe longing hopeless still unspoken unknown
patterns menace and flirt flit again against old *patterns*
dilapidated *patterns*

forced nomadic. My molly rising my molly departing my
molly. And you and you and you. And then.

     Twittering against sharp *patterns*
unannounced departures to haunt to haunt to menace and flirt
broken goodnights not yet three weeks my molly not my molly
goodnight my molly goodbye. Forgetting folksongs

Saturday:

Changed minds crest and fall menace and flirt fritter and
declaim severe monumental *patterns*
motionless twittering. And then. My molly my pollyanna my
beatrice and you and you and you before time out of time
passing again again against severe longing bad poetry again
against *patterns*
of disbelief unrequited fateful *patterns*.

     Twittering. To haunt the feeble memory rushed
missing *patterns*
twittering crushed and hopeless poetry fails unknown unheard
unseen lost again against. And then. And then. Like next week
like last week twittering glib glib glib. pollyanna strikes
indifferent. beatrice strikes indifferent. My molly my molly my
molly my my my indifferent twittering marks mars to haunt
the crowded great room departed

Saturday:

Preparations are made plans are laid plots played pointed
toward tomorrow. Departed. Never next. And then. And you
and you my sweet molly my small molly never again against
patterns
slipping forward untoward the next so sweet to haunt to haunt
to touch.

       Twittering. Uncertain *patterns*
unstable moment to deny denying out of time failing again
against dissipating *patterns*
flood the never next so severe so severe severed longing lost.
Twittering pollyanna twitters worried *patterns*
severe poetry and cynical hope to fallen fury not the next
crests and falls to crest and fall chortling chirp chirp clack
melodious

Sunday:

Please please please my molly to haunt my molly goodnight
my molly. Dishonest hopeless faith severe longing chortling
chattering contrite please please please. Severe *patterns*
longing *patterns*
too many *patterns*

falling failing foolish into cynical hope my pollyanna my
beatrice like last month like yesterday again against tomorrow.
And you. Moments upon moments upon moments.

       Twittering. Blocked by *patterns*
flitting *patterns*
of disbelief severe poetry. And lately. And you. Impossible
sweet unfailing next

Thursday:

Against weak *patterns*
not yet goodbye not yet *patterns*
pollyanna not yet goodbye my molly my molly not my molly
goodbye.

       Twittering nomadic mindful chirping sifting chortled
haunting *patterns*.
To haunt to haunt to haunt to balance lagging time. Contrite
absolution dedicated to faithless fate too frail without. Across
the vacant bedroom severe humorless *patterns*
mindless *patterns*
menace and flirt. Flit flit flit. Against. And you. My molly
rising to forget. And then. And you. Out of time placeless next
out of time now next now next week now tomorrow.

Twittering. Beginning. Against weak ill-fated *patterns*
out of time goodbye my molly hello

Appendix Q.

The Narrator reports that the spark has gone out.

Molly labors to forget Newgate, which has the exact opposite
effect – reminding her of the horrors of this long gone past,
which then produces a feeling of nostalgia throughout her
body, her body of work. Writing, especially in the domain of
the Author, becomes impossibly labored. The desk is
cluttered, pell-mell. The written, especially in the domain of
the Narrator, has become impossibly contrived. The novel is
cluttered, pell-mell. This container holds only the remnants of
rituals (genies in bottles, ghosts in machines), the ruins of what
can be remembered. Excluding all else – everything that
matters. The Narrator, by now, just wants to be left alone.
There is no joy in recalling, and recalling again and again. Too
much has been lost. All the Author can offer of the Narrator
is a reflexive and idiomatic poetics for Molly. The Author's
refusal to provide the Narrator with a satisfactory narrative
context prohibits the novel from becoming the Novel.

The Author reports that the spark has gone out.

Appendix R.

Weakend by the malapropos
knowing

only the lubric solace
of sympathetic perfidy

feeble nightmares wake the dormant

unmoved
inspiration

follows efflorescent toward
numbered daybreaks
surrendered in ascetic fortune

promising
retreat

consistent
abberations

the jovial sobriety of unshakable pastiche

Week Ten

Sunday:

Anticipation haunts the next not the next to haunt to haunt to
haunt my molly haunted. Departed.

Twittering. Forced focused else and anywhere again
against severe longing *patterns*
of faithless poetry tomorrow tomorrow tomorrow. And then.
And you. And then *patterns*
of longing severed waiting lost listless without. And then.

Twittering. Teetering suspicion haunts the next now
and then again against and without listening listing rocking
foot to foot pacing *patterns*
of disbelief severed longing lost.

Twittering. Suspicious *patterns*
crest and fall crest and fall to menace and flirt again against
unspoken. Without poetry moments wither wailing *patterns*
again against my missing molly my departed molly my molly

not my molly. And then. And then desperation falters falling
immediate concern contrition failing flailing discontent

Saturday:

And then my my my.

     Twittering. And then. The momentary possibility
improbable unknown *patterns*
crest and fall and rise again against broken *patterns*
hesitant monuments to haunt to haunt my molly emerges
hopelessly again against *patterns*.

     Twittering. Belligerent and corporeal desperation
severe longing old *patterns*
dead *patterns*
lost *patterns*
stitched to the next the now the next so sweet and then.

     Twittering. Not now. Today tomorrow. And then.

     Twittering. Emotional meander toward untoward
severe thresholds untimely and unhinged monuments already
out of time predicted dilapidated chortle and cynical *patterns*
of hope denied.

Twittering. To need to need to need my molly untimely
challenged hopeless *patterns*
and then. Flit flit flit. And then.

Twittering.

click click click

And then. Now to forget my molly my molly twittering
impatience suffered severe smiles.

Twittering longing as yet as yet and you and you

Wednesday:

Scattered recumbent *patterns*
decumbent faithless faith menace and flirt menace and flirt
again against acknowledged *patterns*
spilt guts reveal my molly unknown my molly impossible my
molly not my molly.

Twittering clack clack click clack clack click. Dull
subjects forget forgotten *patterns*
folksongs to haunt to haunt to haunt the dilapidated vacancy
crowded with my molly my molly my molly. pollyanna chortles
and you and you and you. Static mindless *patterns*

hopeless chirping faithless fated hope and menace and flirt
next and now against uncanny *patterns*
of cynical hope and then. Impossible futures flit forget my
molly unfathomable again

Monday:

To haunt to haunt to haunt tomorrow departed. My molly
twittering my molly forced and frail my molly elsewhere. Again
against severe poetry longing *patterns*
of discontent of disbelief. And you. Severed waiting yesterdays
fall lost and listless chortling tomorrows falter crest and fall
menace and flirt flit between *patterns*
unspoken *patterns*
to haunt to haunt haunting *patterns*.

Twittering. Severe suspicious longing *patterns*
lost and lacking poetry monuments to discontent my molly
departed my molly not my molly and you. And then. And then
cynical hope crests and falls

Sunday:

Echoes rebound forged and silent *patterns*
at rest at work reprised slipping forward out of time to touch
to haunt to haunt to haunt at dawn to haunt at dusk.

Twittering. Hopeless hope and cynical *patterns*
requite slipping forward out of time to touch

click click click

Questions twitter echoing severe disbelief severe longing less
for light snow heavy crystalline cynical hope to haunt to haunt
to haunt crushed and distracted too short days at dawn at dusk
forgotten echoes chirping chortling.

Twittering. Joyful flits fits surge. And then. Severe
thresholds crossing impatient chortling forged forgotten
untimely and unhinged moments denied my molly denies my
molly pretends my molly. Untimely and unhinged

Tuesday:

And then. Hello again. Uncanny *patterns*
revealed spoken large and larger remembered to the moment
and then. And you and you and you my molly.

Twittering. Impossible future filtered response again
against cynical hope forgotten *patterns*
the impossible next and now. The silent *patterns*
transfigured chortling nomadic vacancy of the crowded
barroom and then and you and you and you.

Twittering. Utterly otherly *patterns*
unknowable *patterns*

forged forgotten in time out of time. Again against the
impossible the reasonable severe longing else and then and
you pollyanna and you beatrice and you my molly my molly
my molly. Soft morning victories unspoken sever poetry and
you and then again against unknown *patterns*.

Perfect hopeless twittering

Friday:

The tongue the hand the finger killing timeless time severe
longing deflated. Dawn dusk crest and fall twittering cynical
patterns
menace and flirt hopeless to haunt to haunt to haunt. Tattered.
My molly departed my beatrice departed into silent busy
patterns
hopeless *patterns*
wandering *patterns*
forgotten *patterns*
misfortunate *patterns*.

And then. Light snow and timeless untimely longing severe
poetry

click click click

flirt flicker flit and fade crushed.

      Twittering. Again against chortled *patterns*
of wasted discontent. And you and you and still short days
joyful longing severe twittering hope out of time. Wandering
patterns
then and now again against arc and spark curious and chaotic
patterns
breaking silence. Misfortune forgotten

Appendix S.

I, I, I, I, I, I, I,
I, I, I, I, I, I, I, I. Did we?
We, we, we, we, we, we, we,
we, we, we, we, we, we, we, we. Did we?

The school marm passes again and is much younger than before. The pink sweater was the problem... The left side of her face is much younger than the right. My profile of the original profile (right) was wrong and the left leaves me with a different impression. She is probably a student. Reserved, like a library book.

Evaporation: The thing dethinged. That is to say, predicting the future. Again ... feeling edgy, ludicrous... haunted by options unattainable ... distant *mardröm* ... dull and quiet, chilled... So, I smoke her last cigarette and think I should drink more; my head isn't spinning so I think I can take more. Everything kaleidoscopic, unspoken visions whisper, shift, thinking that at least a proper head spin would offer something different. The cigarette feels good but is not enough of a reminder. The cigarette is good but is not enough to penetrate the Bourbon. The cigarette is good but is not potent enough for me to feel I am really smoking...

Appendix T.

In the park

A beautiful afternoon

in the park with Dostoevsky

with parasol and papa

in the park with Nabokov

follow, follow

in the park with Mallarmé

Look!

in the park with Balzac

a snifter would have done no harm

in the park with Nietzsche and his
sister

Where will this lead us?

in the park with Artaud and his
nurse

to the commons, to the square, the piazza, the arcade

we will continue

On the lam

two kid goats

We are feeling sorry

to plot away from plot

clean white dreams escape

we apologize

back to zero

we begin the inquisition

stubborn   memories   of   forgotten

burdens

we are feeling strong

apologies accepted

now, becoming nomad

Week Eleven

Wednesday:

Twittering. Waiting preternatural *patterns*
uncanny *patterns*
still light snow and then. And you. My molly impossible my
molly panicky my my my departed again and then. And then.

Twittering. Hopeless cynical hope wandering long
wondering and then and now severe longing *patterns*
of misfortune West North North menace and flirt. West
North North menace and flirt to haunt to haunt to haunt
untimely aberrations crest and fall to menace and flirt flit
flicker. Weeks and weeks away forgetting folksongs lost
patterns
mysterious longing severe poetry. And you. And then and now
smiling remembered my molly remembered my molly
departed. And then pollyanna promises

Thursday:

Impossible melancholic *patterns*
worrisome beginnings ill-fated forgotten my molly my molly
my departed molly again against away and hopeless cynical
hope crests and falls weakened by weekend *patterns*.

And then. Severe longing distracted moments of disbelief and
hope and worry and melancholic chortled melodies. Joik.
Untimely twittering impatient *patterns*
trembling *patterns*
chirp chirp chirp. Departing next and now my molly my molly
my molly *patterns*
fade frazzled focus affirms rebuff.

　　　　Twittering. Misfortunate endings menace and flirt again
against time out of time predicted stoic soft hope North
North West South. Lost to moments indulgent *patterns*
indignant *patterns*
old and new *patterns*
of misunderstanding hapless severe chastity dies so sweet
impossible last lost next my molly my molly my molly
impossible. Waiting waning next last lost next fails crushed up
to hope.

　　　　Twittering supressed

Friday:

To need to want to know not now my molly my pollyanna my Beatrice impossible. Slippery dog days long nights and still light snow out of time. And then.

Twittering ill-fated fate frail faithless listless hopeless cynical hope

click click click

Across the table across the crowded great room across again against again. And you. My molly.

Twittering against sleeping daylight *patterns*
goodnight *patterns*
goodbye *patterns*
follow frail twilight chortling *patterns*.

The next not the next so sweet severe poetry and flitting frail twittering *patterns*
fade.

click click click

Chorte chortle chortle. To haunt to haunt to haunt. And then. Unknown and then. And you and you and you not the next so sweet goodbye. Goodnight

Monday:

New *patterns*
old *patterns*
haunt to haunt to figure the next so sweet impossible nexus undetermined.

     Twittering. And you and you and you my molly the next not the next arriving in departure from the faithless fate unreasonable *patterns*
longing *patterns*.

Severe uncanny *patterns*
outside of time despite moments movements monuments revealed and then. And you and you and you arriving in departure again against unfathomable *patterns*
my molly wonders. Distant chortle marked by nepenthean *patterns*
cynical hope crest and fall crest and fall again against vacant eyes wandering across the silent *patterns*
of the crowded barroom.

Twittering my molly in disbelief my molly to forget my molly in future denial. And then.

Twittering. And then.

Twittering. And then despondent severe poetry again against my molly lost. South West North East

Wednesday:

Across the crowded great room haunting *patterns*
forced nomadic mindful chirping.

Twittering chortle haunts to haunt to menace and flirt.
Gathered placeless unknown *patterns*
smiles mirror impossible bodies out of time already again
against. Beginning. Beginnings. my molly rising my molly
arriving now next never next my molly

click click click

And you and you and you. Humorless moments fizzle flitting
patterns
unknowable yet and you and you and you. And then. Too
much frail fated listless without.

Twittering. Against *patterns*
weak not yet two weeks goodbye my molly goodnight

Thursday:

Unhinged *patterns*
and nowhere to eat no place nowhere here and there. And
then.

Twittering.

Twittering memory marks moments monumental
patterns
of untimely discontented *patterns*
again against my molly my molly and pollyanna monuments in
ruins. Lost in Gamla Stan. Lost in Södermalm.

Twittering. Weaving unhinged staggered stepped and
twisted *patterns*
old *patterns*
to haunt to haunt to menace and flirt.

Twittering. Lost and haggard fallen left to transit forged
and severe longing out of time timeless placeless groundless
deep tragic joyful wandering faithless and forgotten weaving
severe longing too much too much too many *patterns*
chattering decline chortling decline chirping decline

144

click click click

No smiling again against like yesterday like last week last month continued

Tuesday:

 None of this will matter.

        Twittering. Out of time and so and then and so and then. Echoed severe longing fades to form monuments of disbelief remains and ashen artifacts my molly departed my molly unrequited my molly filled with cynical hopeless hope and soft worry flits to forget forged *patterns*
of discontent recalled. And then. And then. And then. And you. Severe longing echoes to forge manacles of disbelief ruins and ashen artifacts pollyanna departed pollyanna unrequited pollyanna filled with hopeless cynical hope and soft worry flits to forget forged *patterns*
of discontent recoiled. And then. And then. And then. And you. Severe longing echoes and fades forgotten moments of disbelief and ashen artifacts beatrice remains beatrice recalls cynical hopeless hope and soft worry flits to forge forgotten remote *patterns*
of discontent requited

Appendix U.

Haydn: *Sieben Worte des Erloesers. Introduction: Maestoso Adagio.*

> *(She enters through the back door -- so young, still holding her flower – a lily none-the-less. She ignores everyone, is above it all. She has an urgent task to perform – to mock the old man.) (Pointing at the flower – precocious, yet coy) (Pause) (She rises) (She throws the old man's manuscript into the fire, waits a moment and retrieves it.) (Aside) (She begins to mark-up the manuscript with a red pencil) (She rises) (She sits) (She kisses the bald spot on the top of the old man's head) (She goes to the coat rack and considers pawning the old man's overcoat) (She exits)*

Close to Easter Sunday, Good Friday, the day after, Easter Eve it was, just before sundown, at dusk or a bit later, just after twilight, somewhere, more than half way, between Cambodia and Gamla Stan, among the rubbish of bygone wandering witches, high on a hill, just off Drottninggatan, 21 blocks from Berzelii Park, they, quite by accident, came upon the Titan, the bronze, bullyragging Titan, stretched out and shirtless, resting upon the rigid pedestal, bronze as well, a tombstone really, inscribed with the master's words, the titles of plays, the titles of novels, in full uneasy repose, as if there were something on his mind, haunting his mind, still, haunted, still, and haunting the century old pages, as if born to suffer, prone to fever, fear, and frenzy, a guarded survivor, the Titan, the bronze Titan at rest, as best a titan can rest, Eldh's Titan, the monument to the master, rendered in full, with the trademark moustache, the piercing eyes, idealized, the Titan, shirtless, in uneasy repose, just around the corner from the museum, where the master had lived, where he wrote Faulkner as Eleonora, his last will, the Blue Tower, on Drottninggatan, where the Titan had, after asking for forgiveness, retired and passed on.

Haydn's *Sieben Worte. Largo No. 1.*

> *(She is reading at the kitchen table. The old man is reading at the kitchen table) (She sheds light on the old man) (She rises and places her shawl over the old man's shoulders) (She sheds light on the old man) (She shakes her head) (She and the old man listen to the racket outside the flat) (She rises to speak) (The old man whispers something into her ear) (She tries to speak) (The old man whispers something into her ear) (She listens) (The old man plays the piano) (Listening) (Standing) (Spying) (Laughing)*

Appendix V.

Upright walking new century man

agent of a manic century

side steps toward escalation

I will win

Ka-ching!

cosmo-political new mania man

politico-pillar of the new community

sour grapes and notes

Arbiter of nothing

I wash my hands of it...

Week Twelve

Friday:

Latent longing severe longing bad bad poetry unrequited silent
patterns
screaming *patterns*
my molly my molly my molly anticipated my molly my molly
my molly postponed.

      Twittering. Absent chortle marked again against *patterns*
of ill-fated faithless fate and you and you and you marked by
patterns
of impossible longing severe poetry pollyanna *patterns*
of discontent impossible worry and you.

      Twittering. And then. And then. And then.
      Twittering. And then. And then. And then.
      Twittering *patterns*.

And then *patterns*.
And then *patterns*.

And then *patterns*.
And then

Tuesday:

My molly departed. My molly twittering my molly my molly
my molly crushing presence forced and frail my molly. And
then. Unrequited *patterns*
ill-fated hopeless longing lost moments my molly denies.

      Twittering yesterday last month tomorrow crests and
falls. And you.

      Twittering. And my molly.

      Twittering. And pollyanna twittering. And beatrice glib
glib glib. Prim prim prim. And then misfortune finds quick
patterns
to haunt to menace and flirt flit feeble falling failing faithless
ill-fated *patterns*.

Monuments to discontent severe poetry lack lull fall fail feeble
severe.

      Twittering. Hapless moments crest and fall returned
and unrequited again against better judgment chortling. And
you. My molly my molly my molly menace and flirt suspicious

longing *patterns*
of disbelief. To haunt unspoken

Thursday:

Forgetting pollyanna *patterns*
and then and you and you and you beyond the next and now
against unknown tasks and fateful *patterns*
haunt to haunt the now. Rootless flitting follows scattered
recumbent *patterns*
acknowledged *patterns*
reveal my molly unknown my molly impossible my molly not
my molly. Pollyanna twittering. And you.

Twittering clack clack clack.

click click click

and pollyanna chortling concerns severe longing preternatural
poetry. Impossible melancholic *patterns*
worrisome beginnings ill-fated endings the last the last the
next.

Twittering. And you. Forgetting truncated goodbye
patterns
next and now again against dull subjects impossible futures

clutter and crowd my molly. Misfortunate greetings menace and flirt again against time predicted. And then. North North West South. Lost to indulgent moments indignant *patterns* of misunderstanding hapless hope severe poetry so sweet impossible last lost next my molly my molly my molly unknown.My departed molly again

Monday:

Distant chortle marked again against *patterns* of ill-fated faithless fate and you and you and you marked by *patterns* of impossible longing severe poetry again against *patterns* of impossible longing and you and you and you.

> Twittering. And then.
> Twittering. And then.
> Twittering *patterns*.

And then severe poetry lost again against my molly to menace and flirt crest and fall again against preternatural *patterns* severe *patterns* of discontent.

Twittering. Chortling within despondent silent letters tragic silent signs and songs. Chortling against the monuments of discontent to hope in cynical hope to crest and fall again to crest and fall again against sad affection all misfortune.

Twittering. Dim, then dimmer, then off

Tuesday:

Beatrice. And then. Untimely wicker pigs to haunt to haunt to mence and flirt beatrice departed pollyanna forgotten out of time played again against uncanny severe poetry. Chortling across the crowded great room cynical hopeless hope already familiar uttered *patterns*
impossible *patterns*.

Twittering. Beatrice departed forced nomadic memorials and then severe longing lost to hopeless next the next so sweet not the next so sweet my molly. Again against gathering *patterns*
old *patterns*
dead *patterns*
clicking despondent the hand the finger the tongue.

Twittering. And then. And you. The end and then my molly forgetting folksongs to haunt to haunt to menace and flirt sweet cynical mirrored *patterns*.

South West North East all at once nothing and elegant misfortunate *patterns*
toward my molly my my my. Sweet deliverance sweeping time back and forth out of time. Now.

Twittering. Lost in untouchable time lost on Trossö
lost on Langö to forget my pollyanna beatrice twittering clack
clack click again against dubious *patterns*
not yet my molly. Mud mud mud and you

Thursday:

Forgotten *patterns*
twittering rhythms dangerous melodies buried deep dead again
against my molly my molly my molly and beatrice fidgets.

Twittering. Waking early to too much unchecked
severe longing chortling

click click click

without style styled *patterns*
untimely *patterns*
of hopeless dead fear my molly my molly not my molly. Lost
severe severed *patterns*
remit remembered sweet and bitter moments crush and crest
and fall and crest and fall to menace long long long ago.

Twittering. And then. Volatility. To menace and flirt
menace and flirt flitting forward hapless *patterns*

of faithless disbelief blameless eroded memories commute
embellished

Friday:

Wasted youth remembered *patterns*
and you and you and you. My molly my molly not my molly
and you my beatrice lost. Tattered.

       Twittering. Jittery hands contorted moments silent
patterns
to haunt to haunt to haunt timeless untimely longing. The
tongue the hand the finger again against chortling *patterns*
of discontent cynical hope severe longing. Uncanny *patterns*
menace and flirt flicker fade to haunt twittering again against
hopeless *patterns*
faithless ill-fated *patterns*.

My molly departed my beatrice departed killing timeless time
to menace and flirt severe poetic *patterns*.

Deflated

Appendix W.

Here, finally we recognize the architecture as faulty and unstable. The fourth pillar is missing and has been since the start.

When the Author turned to Molly he thought it would be easy, that the construction of the monument would guarantee an audience. But in this birch-lined grove, narration is the unheard cry of profane isolation. The Author has done his best, but this island is de-sorted.

Appendix X.

hammer
> for philosophy
>> / to build and break

scissors
> for decisiveness
>> / to divide and expiate

axe
> for clear thought
>> / to approve and authorize

pencil
> for the author
>> / to document and notarize

fork
> for nourishment
>> / to pitch and pile

dagger
> for ritual
>> / to avenge and equalize

Week Thirteen

Tuesday:

And then. And you. The end.

Friday:

Slighted. Slap slap slap.

      Twittering backwards to haunt to haunt to haunt my
molly missing my molly pollyanna perfect gone evaporating
patterns
and faithless fate falter falling backwards twittering.

      Twittering. And then. And you. And then *patterns*
of severe longing. And then.

      Twittering. Suspicious next never next now and then
again against and without *patterns*
of disbelief. To think to think to think. Still placeless forgotten
severe longing *patterns*
fade faceless tracing moments the impossibility of next so

sweet never so sweet my molly my molly my molly departed.
Backward *patterns*
severe longing beyond my molly re-emerges to haunt to haunt
to haunt. Stranded silent speaking slipping into cynical hopeful
patterns
wasted time out of time played by time. Tattered

Thursday:

Not yet four weeks not yet my molly goodnight not yet
goodbye. And you and you and you. And then Beatrice. And
then pollyanna. And then. Still unspoken unknown *patterns*
menace and flirt flit across too long nights and heavy snow.

     Twittering memories mark moments movements
monuments to forgotten *patterns*
impossible *patterns*.

My Beatrice. No no no.

     Twittering. Again against gathering *patterns*
mirrored *patterns*
of disbelief. And then. My pollyanna. No no no. To haunt to
haunt and then forget my molly my molly my monuments in
ruins.

click click click

Across the table across the crowded great room across the
barroom across to cross again. Placeless. Groundless severe
longing chattering poetry chortling decline chirping decline to
haunt to haunt the next. Staggered stepped and twisted *patterns*
criss-cross the table wavering unhinged midnight *patterns*
goodnight *patterns*
goodbye. My molly rising

Saturday:

Twittering. And then. My my my. Improbable *patterns*
crest and fall heading elsewhere back again against my molly
my molly my molly. Forever. The end of my molly killing my
molly my my my pollyanna *patterns*
my beatrice *patterns*
stitched to the never next toward untoward severe thresholds
unhinged movements moments and cynical hope denied.

Twittering.

Twittering *patterns*
of ill-fated continuation severe longing lost to severe poetry
lost to haunt to haunt severe severity. And then.

Twittering. My molly dies hopeless again against cynical hope hopeless hope out time forgetting untimely poetry. And you and you and you never so sweet never again against frail *patterns*
sleepless *patterns*
of disgust. Today tomorrow and then.

Twittering. Flit flit flit. And then.

Twittering suppressed. *Patterns*
patterns
patterns

Tuesday:

Days and days lost to restraint lost restraint aberrant *patterns*
lift the lonely caustic faithless fate again against the impossible *patterns*
to haunt to haunt to haunt so sweet twittering misfortune passes passing untimely out of time outside.

Twittering to menace and flirt menace and flirt the volatile monuments and mistakes. Weak *patterns*.

And then. Weeks and weeks to come. And then. And you. Folly forced and fickle fades.

Twittering. Misfortune forgotten and busy silence. Cloying chortled time

click click click

crests and falls to the twittering remains of hope. In disbelief

Tuesday:

Severe longing squandered poetry my molly blocks breaks in sad affection lost losing time to too much too little time to haunt to haunt to haunt. To crest and fall conditional *pattern* ignore the signs despondent signs tragic signs silent signs dilapidated already against reason unreasonable. My memory. My molly. My pollyanna. My beatrice. Sweet lost severe poetry.

Twittering. Clack. click. Nostalgia for misfortune beginning now and then against. And you. And you my molly slipping toward forgotten *patterns* otherly *patterns* utterly at Loggerheads losing severe longing dies impossibly my molly my molly not my molly.

Twittering moments forced forging nothingness

click click click

      Twittering. Menace and flirt and menace and
nothingness departed.

      Twittering. The end. My molly my molly my molly
kills. My molly kills my my my beatrice my my my pollyanna
remembering sweeter *patterns*
blissful *patterns*
broken longing lost to forgetting forgotten

Appendix Y.

Moments die unnourished
passing

into memory fading
burnt by false liquidity

concrete domains of sense lost

fallen
still

made restless by
the absent beauty
of monuments in ruin

spilt
silence

a phantom
evocation

the tragic farce of melting ice cream.

Appendix Z.

I smoke her last cigarette and think of her, missing... Everything kaleidoscopic... I call old American friends just to hear a voice. This moment lacks the human, truly, and is at the root of my current frustration. I wish I had another smoke, even her cigarettes are better than none. I'm not a snob.

Finishing quicker than I should have, the butt snuffed out in the dirty packed snow that populates the balcony ... the cigarette is not enough of a reminder. Too much of a reminder -- of recent silent days... "Too much Bourbon," I think to myself as I waddle, stagger to discard the butt -- waddle, stagger toward the tiny kitchen. Waddle, stagger toward repeating myself. "I'll have another Bourbon."

...
...
...

American TV with subtitles, burnt cheese in a sautée pan, fluorescent lights above ... the refrigerator empty but for coffee and Danish cheese, Mellan Mjölk, mustard and citron mayonnaise...

...
...
...

I return to the photographed eye ... a simulation of the original attraction, the singularity, converged, its color, its shape, its precision... the singularity of the exact moment the photograph was taken. I can't believe I am out of cigarettes.

... couldn't, shouldn't ... write the allegories without thinking ahead ... they must be encoded ahead of time, before being committed to words, images, sounds ... silence, I couldn't hear a thing ... I could hear myself thinking ... alone ... all-day ... I didn't write this ... couldn't ... I couldn't think, too distracted ... lost in something that might happen but assuredly will not ... the problem of impermanence -- of moments forgotten before they can be willed ... couldn't, shouldn't ... so vague still, blurred and floating before dark eyes, swimming ... I got nothing done ... now it is tomorrow.

We never make it to St. Pittsburgh.

I leave my duffel in the grass.

Wednesday:

)